★ **BOOK 3** ★
in the **Classroom 13 Series**

WITHDRAWN

and Terrible

THE FANTASTIC FAME OF
CLASSROOM **13**

By **Honest Lee** & **Matthew J. Gilbert**
Art by **Joelle Dreidemy**

LITTLE, BROWN AND COMPANY
New York • Boston

Copyright © 2017 by Hachette Book Group
CLASSROOM 13 is a trademark of Hachette Book Group, Inc.
Cover and interior art by Joelle Dreidemy.

Cover design by Véronique Sweet. Cover copyright © 2017 by Hachette Book Group, Inc.

Little, Brown and Company
Hachette Book Group
1290 Avenue of the Americas, New York, NY 10104
Visit us at LBYR.com

First Edition: December 2017

Little, Brown and Company is a division of Hachette Book Group, Inc.
The Little, Brown name and logo are trademarks of Hachette Book Group, Inc.

The publisher is not responsible for websites (or their content)
that are not owned by the publisher.

Library of Congress Cataloging-in-Publication Data

Names: Lee, Honest, author. | Gilbert, Matthew J., author. | Dreidemy, Joelle, illustrator.
Title: The terrible and fantastic fame of Classroom 13 / by Honest Lee &
Matthew J. Gilbert ; art by Joelle Dreidemy.
Description: First edition. | New York ; Boston : Little, Brown and Company, 2017. |
Series: Classroom 13 ; book 3 | Summary: Ms. Linda's cousin, the Hollywood agent
Lucy LaRoux, gives each student in Classroom 13 the opportunity to become famous,
but the students learn that with great celebrity comes stage fright, injury, bad press,
and giving up video games.
Identifiers: LCCN 2016051850| ISBN 9780316464574 (hardcover) |
ISBN 9780316464581 (paperback) | ISBN 9780316464598 (ebook) |
ISBN 9780316464604 (library ebook edition)
Subjects: | CYAC: Fame—Fiction. | Celebrities—Fiction. | Schools—Fiction.
|Humorous stories.
Classification: LCC PZ7.1.L415 Ter 2017 | DDC [Fic]—dc23
LC record available at https://lccn.loc.gov/2016051850

ISBNs: 978-0-316-46457-4 (hardcover), 978-0-316-46458-1 (paperback),
978-0-316-46459-8 (ebook)

Printed in the United States of America

LSC-C

10 9 8 7 6 5 4 3 2 1

 CONTENTS

PSSST! HEY, YOU! FOR MY CHAPTER, YOU MIGHT WANT TO REWRITE MY CODE—BACKWARDS.

CHAPTER 1
Unfamous Ms. Linda

When *not*-famous schoolteacher Ms. Linda LaCrosse woke up Monday morning, she decided it would be another boring day. Little did she know how wrong she was.

First, she had been up late grading papers and forgotten to set her alarm. Ms. Linda didn't realize it until her cat bit her nose and woke her up. "I'm going to be late! Again!"

Second, she put her right shoe on her left foot, and her left shoe on her right foot. Then she brushed her hair, put on her clothes, and hopped in the shower. As she rushed to school, she wondered why she was soaking wet.

You might think Ms. Linda was quite silly and *should* be famous, but she was *not*. (Not anymore...) Ms. Linda is not a pop star or a TV actress or a soccer player or a famous writer. (Like me, Honest Lee. What's that? Yes, I *am* too famous!)

But Ms. Linda *is* related to someone who knows lots of famous people—her cousin Lucy LaRoux, who is a very famous agent who works at the Ace Agent Agency in Hollywood.

What's an agent? Well, agents are the people who represent pop stars and TV actresses and soccer players and famous writers. They help them get work and help them stay famous. They also charge a great deal of money for their services. (Make a mental note, as this will be important later.)

"Ms. Linda! You are late again!" said the principal. His arms were crossed, and he was tapping his shoe against the floor tiles.

"I know, I know!" Ms. Linda said. She ran past him and straight to her class. As you might know, the students of the 13th Classroom can be quite a handful. And so Ms. Linda expected them to be causing trouble. Instead, she found them all sitting quietly, listening to a story told by someone sitting on her desk.

"...and so I said, 'Don't you dare!' And do you know what Ten Bears did? He ate the entire tarantula."

The whole class laughed.

"Though bears prefer honey, I suppose one would eat a spider," Ms. Linda said. "How is that funny?"

"No, Ms. Linda," said Teo. "*Ten Bears* isn't an

actual bear. He's a human boy and he's *famous*! I want to be just like him."

"What's he famous for?" Ms. Linda asked.

"For being on the Internet," Teo said.

"But *what* is he famous for?" Ms. Linda asked. "What does he *do?*"

"He makes videos. On the Internet," Teo said.

"I don't understand this generation," Ms. Linda said.

"And that's why you're *not* a famous agent like me," said Lucy LaRoux, famous agent of Ace Agent Agency.

"Lucy?! What are you doing here?" Ms. Linda said, surprised to see her cousin outside of Hollywood.

"Well, my boss said we needed more kid stars, and I thought to myself, *Where do I find a bunch of brats—ur, I mean, children?* Naturally I thought of you. You work with children, so here I am. I plan to make all these kids famous!"

The students in Ms. Linda's class screamed with glee. (Except for Yuna. She had no interest in being famous.)

Of Ms. Linda's twenty-seven students, twenty-six of them were present. Not so surprisingly, Santiago was out again. (He wasn't exactly "sick," but his mom insisted he go to the hospital—just because one of his fingers *fell off* his hand. He didn't think it was that big of a deal, but his mother quite disagreed.)

Of the twenty-six students who were in class, twenty-five of them were paying attention to the famous agent who worked at Ace Agent Agency. They never paid this much attention to Ms. Linda. She crossed her arms.

"Lucy, this is a classroom," Ms. Linda said. "You can't just walk in here and distract my students. They are here to learn. Not become famous."

"Can't we do both?" Ava asked.

"I don't know...." Ms. Linda answered.

"You don't want to hold them back, do you?" Lucy asked. "Just because *your* fifteen minutes of fame didn't work out—"

"Ms. Linda was famous?!" Jayden Jason asked, shocked.

"For what?!" asked Chloe.

"She hasn't told you?" Lucy asked. "Well, let me fill you in...."

CHAPTER 2
Infamous Ms. Linda

Once upon a time, little Linda LaCrosse was the same age as her students. And more than anything, she loved to sing. She sang when she did her chores. She sang when she brushed her teeth. She even sang when she slept.

One day, her family went for a visit to Holly-wood, and an agent heard her singing. "What a beautiful singing voice you have!" he said. "I am certain I can make you an opera star!"

And he did.

Little Linda LaCrosse became quite famous. She sang at very important opera houses all around the world. She even got a singing coach. This coach pushed her to sing harder and deeper and higher. It turned out little Linda LaCrosse could sing so high that it made glass break.

Well, at the peak of her fame, she was sent to Beijing, China, to sing at the National Grand Theater—which was made entirely of glass. Her coach kept telling her, "You have to sing harder and deeper and higher than ever before!"

And so she did.

And the entire opera house shattered.

"And *that* was the end of Ms. Linda's singing career," Lucy explained, finishing her story.

"That's wonderful!" said Liam.

"That's horrible," said Ximena.

"I think it's neat," said Lily.

"The famous painter Andy Warhol once said,

'In the future, everyone will be world-famous for fifteen minutes.' And that was *my* fifteen minutes of fame," said Ms. Linda. "Sometimes being famous can quickly lead to being *infamous*."

"Isn't that the same thing?" William asked.

"Not at all," Ms. Linda said. " 'Famous' means being known for something good. 'Infamous' means being known for something *bad*."

"It's better to be infamous than not famous at all," said Preeya.

"Oh, I quite disagree," Ms. Linda said. "I'm still not allowed back into China after what I did."

"Enough talking about you," Lucy LaRoux said. "It's time to make these children celebrities."

"I don't think that's a good idea," Ms. Linda said to her cousin.

"On the contrary." Lucy smiled. "You just said in the future, everyone would be famous for fifteen minutes. Well, the future is now. Who wants to be famous?"

The entire class—except Yuna—cheered and shouted with excitement.

"Fantastic! All of you step right up and sign this contract that makes ~~you my servants~~ me your agent, and we'll get started on making each of you famous."

"What's the contract say?" Ms. Linda asked her cousin. She tried to read the fine print, but it was itsy-bitsy-teeny-tiny....

"Don't worry about it!" Lucy snapped.

Ms. Linda begged the students not to sign the contracts. But as students often do with their teachers, no one listened.

CHAPTER 3
Jayden Jason

Jayden was excited about being famous. He didn't know what he'd be famous for, but he figured Lucy would know. And she did.

"You must be Jayden Jason James, aka Triple J," Lucy said with a sly smile. "I hear you're the most popular kid in school and have a huge following online. I see you also have an undeniable star quality about you. Let's do lunch."

"Doing lunch" in Hollywood means making

deals at a fancy outdoor café with caviar and paparazzi. Here in school, it means making deals at the cafeteria with day-old fish sticks and that one weird kid from Classroom 10 watching them eat.

"Now, I want the *Triple* in Triple J to mean something. Do you know what a 'triple threat' is?" Lucy asked. Jayden shook his head and ate a fish stick.

"It means you're famous for three things instead of one. You can sing *and* act *and* model. Maybe you could act in a movie about a model who sings! Maybe you could even write the movie, do the soundtrack, and design the clothes. What do you think about fragrance? If you can do seven things, you could be a *septuple* threat!"

"Sure, I can do whatever," Jayden said.

Dollar signs lit up in Lucy's eyes.

And somehow Jayden did do it all—*and* he made it look easy.

Triple J wrote his first screenplay that night. The next morning, he filmed all his movie scenes. That afternoon, he recorded his first album, then began to design clothes for his new fashion label. After that, he took a private jet to Italy to model in his first fashion show the next morning. He was a natural.

Within a week, he was bigger than a star—he was a global phenomenon.

His brand name—Triple J—was in magazines, in TV commercials, on the Internet, in movies, everywhere. In almost no time at all, he became a *tredecuple* threat. Meaning, he had *thirteen* different talents. It's almost as if he had *clones* helping him out.

If you've ever seen his movie, the credits say:

A TRIPLE J PRODUCTION STARRING **TRIPLE J**
IN A FILM BY **TRIPLE J** ORIGINAL SOUNDTRACK BY **TRIPLE J**
AND ORIGINAL DANCE CHOREOGRAPHY BY **TRIPLE J**
EDITED BY **SOME WEIRDO**
PRODUCED, DIRECTED, AND CATERED BY **TRIPLE J**

Yes, Triple J could do anything. He'd even gone into the catering business. In between filming scenes, he grilled omelets for the local homeless shelter. "Triple cheese omelets coming right up!" he'd say.

He quickly became Lucy's biggest money-maker. The new deals were pouring in and were going to make ~~Jayden~~ Lucy rich! All Triple J had to do was sign a new contract.

"No thanks," Triple J said.

Lucy nearly choked on her triple grilled cheese. "What?!"

"I'm tired of the biz. Feeding the homeless has shown me there are more important things in life than starring in movies and recording hit records and sleeping on big piles of money. Giving is truly better than getting."

Lucy was furious. "You have lost it! You can't just leave! You can't quit! I have you under contract!"

"So sue me." He laughed. Lucy tried, but Triple J had given all his money to charity, hopped on a plane to Tibet, and become a monk.

There, he learned to meditate. But after a few weeks of absolute quiet, he became absolutely bored. So he came home.

CHAPTER 4
Preeya

"**W**ho's next?" famous agent Lucy LaRoux asked.

Preeya stood on her desk and addressed the room: "I am! I'm the prettiest girl in class..." (This was not true.)

"...and one of the smartest," she continued. (Nor was this.)

"...and I normally tell you guys everything

about my life…" (This *was* true, though most of the students found it quite irritating.)

"…but I've been keeping a major secret from all of you for quite some time," Preeya said. "I'm ready to come clean. I can actually SING! Yes! Me! Just when you thought I couldn't be any more talented or gorgeous or wonderful, here I am, rocking you through song!"

Preeya began to sing. Many of the students covered their ears, expecting to hear a voice like nails on the chalkboard. Instead, everyone was impressed. Preeya was good. Not amazing, mind you, but decent. Lucy saw potential— meaning, she didn't think Preeya was a natural talent, but she could certainly be *molded* into something.

"I'm ready to be a star!" Preeya announced.

First, Lucy phoned the Ace Agent Agency and had them set up some tour dates. Second, she had Preeya record an album and leak it online.

And third, Lucy booked an appointment with famous fashionista Farrah Far-Out-There.

"Why'd you call Farrah? I already have a look!" Preeya said.

"Oh, dollface," Lucy said, "in today's media industry, it's not enough to be a good singer. You have to have a *gimmick* if you want to keep trending."

"What's going to be my gimmick?" Preeya asked.

"Fashion, fashion, fashion!" Lucy said.

For Preeya's first round of public appearances, Farrah Far-Out-There made a dress entirely of raw poultry and fish. Chicken cutlets made her blouse while shiny fish made up her skirt. She wore anchovy earrings and bracelets made of chicken sausage. Preeya felt disgusting, but she smiled for the cameras.

Sophia and Chloe showed up—to boycott her animal-carcass fashion. The next day, Preeya and her chicken-fish dress sizzled all over social media.

Farrah Far-Out-There's next crazy outfit for Preeya was simple: It was a beehive dress—made of an actual beehive with actual bees living inside it. The bees stung Preeya over and over. But once again, she smiled for the cameras.

Sophia and Chloe showed up again—this time to boycott her abuse of bees. This only helped the buzz. Preeya's song "Queen Bee" made number one on the charts.

Next, Farrah Far-Out-There designed a dress made out of jellyfish and porcupines. "Noooooope!" Preeya said. "No way. I don't mind some pain, but that's going too far."

Instead, Farrah Far-Out-There crafted a suit made of 100 percent authentic New York City garbage. She stitched together rotten banana peels, used Chinese-food cartons, and pieces of gum scraped off the sidewalks.

Sure enough, the paparazzi fought in a photo frenzy over Preeya's hot *trash du jour* look. She stunk up the red carpet with it, posing for pic after pic. She may have smelled like a landfill, but the only thing that filled her nostrils was the sweet smell of success.

Finally, it was time for Preeya to take the stage. The lights came up, the crowd roared, and that's when she looked out at all those faces....

Preeya suddenly couldn't move.

All those people. Staring. At her.

There had to be forty thousand eyeballs looking straight at her. Some of them weren't even blinking. Preeya felt like she was about to faint. This wasn't like singing in the shower or performing for her classmates at school—this was different. This was TOO. MANY. PEOPLE.

Preeya instantly remembered why she kept her singing talents hidden—because she had terrible *stage fright*.

She dropped the microphone, ran off stage, and never came back out.

CHAPTER 5
Dev

Dev ran up to Lucy and waved his fingers in front of her face. "Check it out," he said. "Pretty amazing, huh?"

"What am I looking at?" Lucy asked.

"My fast fingers," Dev said. "I'm the best video game player on this side of the planet. Can you make me famous now?"

"What else can you do?" Lucy asked.

"Um...I can play piano."

Dev took a seat at the classroom piano and began playing. He was so good, it brought tears to Ms. Linda's eyes. It turned out that years and years of playing video games had made Dev's fingers incredibly strong, fast, and agile. (He also happened to be a musical prodigy.)

"Now we're cooking." Lucy smiled. "I'm thinking Carnegie Hall."

Dev auditioned, and the classical music judges wept. They agreed to let him play every night of the week—for the rest of his life.

To keep his fingers as nimble as possible, the Ace Agent Agency hired a piano coach. He was an old Russian man named Vladimir Vliolin, and he had a reputation for being strict.

How strict? Well, for starters, Vladimir told Dev he was no longer allowed to play video games.

"WHAT?!" Dev asked, freaking out. "But games are my life!"

"No. Music is life now! Your precious fingers

must rest when they not play piano," Vladimir insisted. "Video games in zee trash!"

So Dev did the sensible thing....

"I quit," he told Lucy.

"But you haven't even played one show yet," she growled. "Your music career hasn't even started! You're not even technically famous. And most important, I haven't gotten any money yet!"

Dev didn't care. Not when the hottest new game of the year was waiting for him at home. Tonight would be an all-night gaming marathon of *Teddy Bear Bashers: Space Capades 2: Comet Cubs*. He cracked his fingers and stretched. Being famous just wasn't as fun as playing video games.

CHAPTER 6
Yuna

Yuna did *not* want to be famous. Ms. Linda told her cousin this, but Lucy LaRoux didn't believe it. She said, "Everyone wants to be famous for something!"

Yuna wrote on a piece of paper and held it up. It said: *I DON'T*.

"Come on, kid," Lucy LaRoux said. "Don't play games with me. What do you want to be famous for? Tell me!"

Yuna scribbled something on a piece of paper and handed it to Lucy. This is what her note said:

.EM OT NOITNETTA DETNAWNU
GNIWARD ERA UOY .ESAELP YAWA
OG WON .SKNAHT ON .HAEY OS
.TUO SI YTIRBELEC A GNIEB
SNAEM TAHT .EM EZINGOCER
NAC ENO ON ,YAD ENO YPS DOOG
A EB OT GNIOG MA I FI DNA
,YPS A EB OT TNAW I .YLLAUTCA
ETISOPPO EHT ETIUQ TNAW I
.SUOMAF EB OT TNAW TON OD I

Lucy threw her hands up. "Fine! Then I give up!" As she wandered away to find a student who *did* want to be famous, Yuna sat back and smiled.

CHAPTER 7
Benji

Benji got dressed up for his meeting with Lucy. Instead of just wearing the clothes he came to school in, he slipped out to his locker for an outfit change. When it was his turn, Lucy found him sporting head-to-toe "football" gear.

Benji spit out his mouth guard and said, "I love two things: unicorns and football. But since there's already a world-famous unicorn, I want to be a famous football player!"

"But you're not wearing a football uniform." Lucy snorted. "You're wearing a *soccer* uniform."

Benji rolled his eyes. "Americans call it soccer, but the rest of the world calls it football. FIFA stands for *Fédération Internationale de Football Association*. One day, I dream of playing in the FIFA World Cup."

Lucy checked the calendar on her phone. "We better hurry, then. The World Cup is this weekend."

That weekend, famous agent Lucy LaRoux escorted Benji to Brazil for the final games of the tournament. Tens of thousands of ~~soccer~~ football fans sat in sold-out arenas, anxiously awaiting the first kick.

Lucy used her Ace Agent Agency connections to get Benji on the roster and in the game. He was now playing for Brazil. When Benji ran out onto the field, his heart swelled with pride. Sure, Benji didn't have muscle, skill, or years of ~~soccer~~ football experience—but he didn't let that bother him. He was about to play professional ball with his heroes.

As the Germans (the opposing team) took the field, they looked at Benji. Some laughed, others growled, and one said, "You're dead meat."

Benji gulped.

His teammates gave him a look of concern. The central midfielder said, "Good luck, kid."

As the referee blew the whistle, the game began. After almost two whole minutes playing the game, the striker kicked the ball to Benji. This was the happiest moment of Benji's young life.

And that was the last thing Benji remembered before everything went black.

Benji woke up in a hospital in a head-to-toe full-body cast. Little Benji got *destroyed* out there.

That's what happens when an untrained kid gets stomped by hundreds of pounds of professional German ~~soccer players~~ footballers.

He broke nearly every single bone in his body. So why was he smiling? His team had won. And since he was technically on the team—even if only for one hundred and twenty seconds—they let him have the trophy. It shined brighter than anything he'd ever seen.

CHAPTER 8
Mason

"I want to be a famous actress!" Mason said. Mason was very good at sports. But he wasn't so bright.

"You mean an *actor*," Lucy said.

"No way. Actresses get all the best roles and win big awards. That's what I want," Mason said.

"But you're a *boy*," Lucy explained to Mason.

"So?!" Mason said, offended. "Boys can be actresses, too!"

Lucy shrugged. "Fine. Let's get your headshot."

Mason ducked under his desk. "What?! Don't shoot me!"

"No, a 'headshot' is just a picture of your face. All actors—and actresses—have them. I send them out to different studio people. Whoever likes your headshot invites you to try out for a role."

"I like bread rolls," Mason said, "with lots of butter."

"Right," Lucy said.

Mason wasn't the smartest (or sharpest) tool in the shed, but he was photogenic. As soon as Lucy sent out his headshot, he got invited to try out for over a dozen TV shows.

Unfortunately, Mason couldn't act his way out of a box. And I mean that very seriously. On his first audition, he got stuck inside a box for thirty minutes and couldn't find his way out.

"Just take the box off your head!" Lucy snapped. She was very frustrated.

At Mason's next audition, he got stuck in

another box. At the third TV set, he followed a cat into a box, and they both got stuck. Some of the film crew started shooting videos of Mason. They couldn't stop laughing.

"This is hilarious!" one of the camera people said. "This should be on the Internet."

This gave Lucy a great idea. She put Mason on the Internet. He was going to be huge. They'd give him his own channel. Maybe they could call it Box Boy.

At the end of the week, Lucy called Mason. "I'm afraid I can't represent you. You're just not fame material. You only got fourteen views on social media. That's less than my goldfish."

"Fourteen views," Mason said. "*Fourteen* views on the *Interwebs?!*" He started jumping up and down and screaming. *"I'm famous! I'm famous. Four. Teen. Views! Mom, I'm a famous actress!!"*

"Of course you are, dear," his mom said.

Lucy hung up the phone.

CHAPTER 9
Isabella

Isabella was very strong. Not normal strong, like kids who like to play outside or exercise. I mean action-hero strong. I suppose that's what happens when you spend all your free time at the stables, wrangling wild horses and riding bulls.

"I want to be a pro wrestler," Isabella told Lucy.

"I like it! Girl power!" Lucy said. "Have you thought of what your wrestler name will be?"

"They'll call me DIZZABELLA—because I'll hit you so hard, I'll make you DIZZY!"

"All right! Time to wrestle some money into *my* bank account!" Lucy said before quickly correcting herself. "I mean, *your* bank account! We're doing this for you. Um, let's go!"

To protect her identity (and hide the fact that she was a minor), Isabella wore a *luchador* mask—a colorful disguise made famous by wrestlers in Mexico and other Spanish-speaking countries.

The Ace Agent Agency arranged Dizzabella's first match against Body Slam Sam. When Dizzabella entered the ring, people laughed at her small size. Body Slam Sam was more than five times bigger than her.

But once the bell rang, it didn't matter. Dizzabella slapped Sam silly and then body-slammed him so hard, he farted a hole right through his wrestling shorts. The crowd was now chortling at him.

When the bell rang, Dizzabella could hardly believe she'd beaten the farts out of a three-hundred-pound muscleman.

"Wow, that was...*easy*," she told the TV cameras.

"You heard it here first, folks!" the ring-side reporter told TV viewers. "Dizzabella says destroying Body Slam Sam was easy!"

After her surprise win, the Pro Wrestling Association invited Dizzabella to compete in the championship match against undefeated champ Dr. Dynamite, the circuit's baddest bad boy. The match took place in Las Vegas, in an arena of fifty thousand wrestling fans—and eleven people who just happened to be there for the all-you-can-eat pancake buffet.

When she heard the bell, Dizzabella charged.

She went with the Mongolian forehead chop. It barely grazed Dr. Dynamite, yet he crashed to the ground. "Please don't hurt me anymore, Dizzabella! Please!" he begged.

Dizzabella looked at her hands. Was she that strong? She paused for a moment, thinking of how odd it all was. *This weakling is the world champ*, she thought. *Earl the Hamster is tougher than this clown.*

Wrestler after wrestler, she defeated with ease. But with each win, she began to suspect something wasn't right—she just couldn't place her finger on it.

Before she knew it, the title bout was down to Dizzabella and her personal wrestling hero, Mountain Man Maniac McGee. There was no way she could take him down. He was a giant!

But Dizzabella had her eyes on the prize: the golden championship belt. If she wanted to wear it, she knew she had to keep fighting.

As soon as the bell rang, Dizzabella used the ropes like a slingshot to fling herself forward. She missed Maniac McGee on the first pass, but she climbed the ropes, did a corkscrew shooting star press, and knocked him so hard that he spun over the ropes and crashed facedown into the maple syrup bucket at the buffet line. He was knocked out cold.

The entire audience stood and cheered. Except for the eleven people who were just there for the pancakes. They were upset about the spilled syrup.

The announcer held Dizzabella's arm up in the air and proclaimed, "Your new heavyweight champion of the worrrrrld: DIZZABELLA!!"

They gave her the giant gold belt. It was the happiest moment of her life. So why was something bothering her?

Lucy pulled her backstage. "You did great, kid! We have endorsements coming out the wazoo!"

"I can't believe it was so easy to beat Maniac McGee," Dizzabella said.

"I can," Lucy said. "It's all fake! There was no way you were going to lose!"

"WHAT?!"

"All that body-slamming and kicking? Fake. The tension between rivals? Fake. Heck, even this gold belt? Fake! The winners are all decided beforehand. Good thing they picked you to win, huh?"

Isabella couldn't believe the whole thing was staged. She felt like such a fraud. She wanted to win for real, not for fake.

So she body-slammed Lucy. For real.

CHAPTER 10
Santiago

You're probably wondering why Santiago's finger fell off. I'll tell you.

Most of the time, Santiago was sick, sneezing, snotting, and snoring all over the place. But for once, he woke up and felt great. The medicines his doctors prescribed hadn't worked, but his grandma's famous chicken soup sure had. His recent flu/cold/allergy thing was finally gone.

"I'm actually hungry today!" he told his mom. "Can I have a sandwich instead of soup today?"

"Of course," his mom said. "Give me just one minute, and I'll make it for you."

"I can make it!" Santiago said.

"Why don't you let me make it?" his mom asked. "Your father just had the knives sharpened the other day, and they're very sharp."

"I'll be careful," Santiago said.

Except that he wasn't careful. He was watching TV while he made his sandwich. So when he went to cut the crust off his sandwich, well...

...instead...

...he cut off...

(you know)

...HIS FINGER.

Ouch.

Don't worry. They sewed it back on. It's as good as new. Except for the uncontrollable twitching—which makes picking his nose very difficult.

CHAPTER 11
Sophia

Sophia is a tree hugger. That means she hugs trees. Literally.

But she also protects them. And not just trees, but animals and oceans and grass and pretty much anything on the planet that is natural.

So when Lucy asked her what she wanted to be famous for, Sophia smiled wide and said, "I want to save the planet."

"I like it," Lucy said. "Go with it!"

The Ace Agent Agency drove Sophia to a local construction site where they were tearing down a forest to put up a new business building. When Sophia saw this, she was furious. She shouted, "What did these woods ever do to you?!"

Sophia was so angry, she chained herself to the trees. "You can't knock down the rest of the forest without running me over. So take that!"

Within an hour, every news crew in the state had showed up to interview Sophia. "I just want to help clean up the world," Sophia explained. That night, she let all the air out of the tractor tires.

"I was expecting a peaceful protest," Lucy said, "but this works even better."

Next, the Ace Agent Agency flew Sophia to an oil field where they were drilling for oil. Once again, she chained herself up. This time, she yelled, "Quit stealing from the earth!" Once again, the news crews showed up to interview her. And that night, she gunked up all the drills with lots and lots of chewing gum.

After that, the Ace Agent Agency boated her to a fishing village, where she put on a scuba suit and chained herself to the fishing boats. "Leave the little fishies alone!" she shouted. News crews came again. With so many cameras watching her, Sophia felt something *snap*! Overcome with rage, she sank the fishing boats. And it was all caught on film.

The next morning, Lucy called her up and said, "Great news on the news! You're famous! They're calling you the Eco-Warrior."

Sophia read the headline:

ECO-WARRIOR TERRORIZES LOCAL FISHING TOWN. SINKS BOATS AND PUTS WORKERS OUT OF WORK.

"Oh no," Sophia said. "I didn't mean to make people lose their jobs!"

"But it's helping the planet!" Lucy said. "You want to help the planet, don't you?"

"I guess so," Sophia said, not so sure.

"Well, people all over the world are looking to you for the next step in saving the planet. I'm

thinking Eco-Warrior T-shirts and Eco-Warrior posters and... how about an Eco-Warrior Million Person March?! You can march to the nation's capital and demand better treatment of plants."

"If it will help the earth..." Sophia said.

So the next week, Sophia arrived in Washington, D.C., by helicopter. There, she led a Million Person March to save the planet. But as the millions of people marched toward the Capitol, Sophia saw they were trampling the grass.

"Walk on the sidewalks!" Sophia shouted, but no one heard her. They were protesting too loudly.

By the time the millions of people had finished their march, they had killed the grass *and* left a trail of trash behind them.

"What have I done?!" Sophia yelled in anguish. For the next several weeks, Sophia cleaned up the trash, replanted every blade of grass that had been destroyed, and told Lucy she quit. She tore up her contract—and then recycled it.

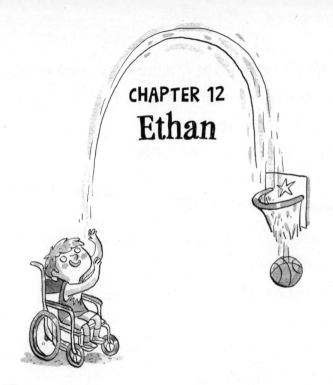

CHAPTER 12
Ethan

Famous agent Lucy LaRoux was annoyed with these kids quitting on her. She didn't understand how wanting to lead a happy, normal life was more important than money. It was a ridiculous notion. She took a deep breath and went to the next student.

Now, if you know Ethan, you know he has a hard time making up his mind. When he found out he could be famous for something, he immediately thought of two different things but couldn't decide which.

"I either want to be a basketball player or a daredevil stuntman," Ethan explained to Lucy. "What do you think I would be better at?"

"Seriously?" Lucy asked. "Um, neither. You're in a wheelchair."

"EXCUSE ME?!" Ms. Linda and Sophia and Benji and Isabella and Mark roared at Lucy at the same time. They all crossed their arms and glared at her in outrage.

"Ethan can be anything he wants to be!" Ms. Linda said.

"And he can do anything he wants to!" Sophia added.

"You're a horrible person," added Benji.

"I agree. I *am* horrible!" Lucy smiled. "That's what makes me such a good agent. As for you, Ethan, let's go with daredevil stuntman. Show me what you've got."

With Ace Agent Agency's help, Ethan arranged a series of stunts, each bigger than the next.

First, he went down the highest roller coaster in the world—in his wheelchair. Next, he jumped over twenty cars and through twelve hoops of fire—in his wheelchair. After that, he walked a tightrope between two skyscrapers, eighty stories up—in his wheelchair.

Finally, he jumped out of a plane over Mount Everest in a wingsuit (you know, those things that make people look like they're flying squirrels) and flew all the way down to the base of the mountain, where he landed gracefully—in his wheelchair.

People all over the world watched Ethan's videos. They clapped and cheered and sent him emails asking how he did it. People made T-shirts and asked for his autograph. The whole time, Ethan was in his head, wondering if he'd made the right choice. After all, being a daredevil stuntman was cool, but playing basketball was even cooler.

"I guess you proved me wrong," Lucy said. "Good job. Looks like we're going to be in business together for a long time. What do you want to do next?"

"Continue proving you wrong," Ethan said. "Let's go play basketball."

CHAPTER 13

Classroom 13

For some odd reason, Lucy LaRoux, famous agent of Ace Agent Agency, didn't even consider representing Classroom 13. The 13th Classroom tried to speak up and say it wanted to be famous, but the students (as usual) were being far too loud.

Filled with jealousy and rage, the 13th Classroom vowed revenge (for the third time) on all of Ms. Linda's students and also that terrible Lucy LaRoux. . . .

CHAPTER 14
Ximena

As Lucy looked for her next ~~victim~~ client, she found Ximena sitting at her desk quietly sketching flowers.

"What do you want to be famous for?" Lucy asked. "What's your talent?"

"I don't have any talent," Ximena said. (Which was a silly thing to say, as every child is good at something, whether they know it or not.)

"Everyone has something that can be ~~exploited~~ used," Lucy said. "For instance, your art. Let me see those sketches...."

"I like to draw flowers," Ximena said as Lucy flipped through her sketchbook. Each and every page was covered in sketches of flowers.

"I've seen enough," Lucy said. "You're coming to New York City with me. Time for the modern art world to meet their newest sensation: Ximena!"

Once Ximena got to New York City, Lucy put her up in a studio and told her to draw until she couldn't feel her hand. And that's exactly what Ximena did. She drew big flowers and small flowers. She sketched fat flowers and skinny flowers. She painted bright flowers and dark flowers.

After only a week, she'd made thousands of pictures of flowers. Lucy LaRoux framed them and put them up in a gallery. They were going to have the biggest art opening ever....

Ahem. Can I interrupt the story for a second? Believe it or not, your ol' pal Honest Lee here has been to a few art openings and knows a thing or two about the snooty art world. Let me explain how it works for you:

There is *free* cheese at art openings. Eat as much as you want. There's always more. Don't let them tell you otherwise. Even if they say, "Honest Lee, leave some for the other patrons!" Eat all you want. Cheese is awesome—unless of course you're lactose intolerant.

It was Ximena's big night, so she wore her favorite flower dress, which her *abuela* had made for her. She only expected maybe twenty people to show up for her show. Instead, hundreds came! There was a line out the door of people trying to get in. The art world loved her flowers. And, more important, they loved Ximena.

"She's so nice," they said.

"And easy to talk to," others said.

"And her art? The flowers are more real than...real flowers!"

Millionaires paid millions for her artistic renderings of flowers. "I can't even tell what kind of flower this is," one rich man said, "which means it's obviously the best and I need to buy it at any cost."

"Sold!" Lucy shouted, counting the piles of cash.

Yes, art types and critics alike loved Ximena's portraits of flowers. She was the newest artist of her age, and the best part was, this was only the beginning.

The next day, Lucy said, "Okay, things in the art world are always moving and changing, so what are you going to draw next?"

"More flowers, I guess," Ximena said. "That's all I know how to draw."

"Surely you can do more than just flowers," Lucy said. "Try to draw a person. Or a puppy. Or some stars!" Ximena drew a person, a puppy, and some stars. But they all looked like flowers.

"Try a robot, or a cowboy, or some skulls!" Lucy said. Ximena drew a robot, a cowboy, and some skulls. They all looked like flowers, too.

"Try a house, or an ocean, or some saltine crackers!" Ximena drew a house, an ocean, and some saltine crackers. They, too, all looked like flowers.

"I give up," Lucy said.

"Oh, I can do kittens!" Ximena said.

"Yes, do that!"

Ximena drew a kitten, but it looked like a flower, too.

"If you can't draw anything else, your art career is over," Lucy said. Ximena shrugged. She didn't mind. She really liked drawing flowers.

CHAPTER 15
Hugo

*B*ien qu'Hugo était français, il avait toujours adoré la musique country américaine. Cette musique parlait de courage, de grand amour et aussi de barbecue, qu'il adorait. Ses chanteurs préférés venaient du Texas, d'Alabama et de Géorgie. Et il pensait que les vieux westerns étaient les meilleurs films.

Alors, lorsqu'il a pu essayer de devenir célèbre, il a tout de suite su ce qu'il voulait être : un chanteur de country! Hugo jouait de la guitare et écrivait des chansons depuis qu'il avait cinq ans. Cela impressionna Lucy, qui le mit sur la scène du Grand Ole Opry à Nashville dans le Tennessee. Malheureusement, comme toutes les chansons d'Hugo étaient en français, personne ne pouvait comprendre le moindre mot de ce qu'il chantait.

CHAPTER 16
Ava

"And what are *you* good at?" Lucy asked Ava.

"Well, I'm a really good friend, and I like animals, and I play tennis really good—" Ava started.

"*Well,*" Ms. Linda corrected. "You don't play *good*, you play *well*."

"Right," Ava said. "I play *well*. *Weller* than most. I'm the *wellest* at tennis."

"That's *not* grammatically correct," Ms. Linda said.

"Who cares about grammar?" Lucy said. "Can't you see this kid is going to be a famous tennis player?!"

The next thing Ava knew, she was playing at the Australian Open in Melbourne. It turns out Ava really was the *wellest* at tennis. She beat everyone in the outback—even a kangaroo.

She was exhausted. (She hated naps, but for the first time in her life, she really wanted nothing more than to take one.)

After that, Ava flew to the French Open in Paris. She'd never been to Paris before, and she couldn't wait to see the Louvre museum. She played game after game—and won each time. "Can I go see the Louvre now?" Ava asked after she won first place.

"Not right now," Lucy said. "You need to keep playing tennis if you want to be famous for it."

Ava flew to the US Open in New York City. Ava's uncles lived there, and the rest of the family came to see her. Everyone was excited to have a family reunion. "You can see them after you win," Lucy said. So Ava played and played and played. Once again, she won first place.

But Lucy had a plane waiting for her. "You'll have to see your family next time. You got an invitation to play in the Wimbledon Championships in London. You can't say no!"

Ava felt terrible. "I miss my family and I'm tired of playing tennis."

"Do you want to be known as the world's *wellest* tennis player?" Lucy asked.

"Yeah, I think so," Ava answered, now unsure.

"Then you have to keep playing."

Ava flew to London. There, she beat every famous tennis player, male and female, in the whole world. But before they gave her the title of the *Wellest Tennis Player in the Whole World*,

one more person wanted to play her—the queen of England!

"I can't beat the queen in tennis!" Ava said, thinking of her own lovely grandmother Shirley. "That would be rude!"

"Don't you want to be famous?!" Lucy shouted.

Ava thought about it. She really did like tennis, but maybe it wasn't worth embarrassing the queen of England. Plus, she missed her family, especially her cousins—Angelina, Siena, Sophia, Taylor, and Morgan. Ava was surprised to find she even missed her brother.

"I'm done with fame," Ava said. She handed her tennis racket to Lucy and went home.

CHAPTER 17
William

Lucy LaRoux was a Hollywood agent. That meant she usually judged people based purely on looks. So when she saw William Wilhelm, she said, "Puny, short, wears glasses...you must be the class genius!"

"What? Who? Me?" William said. "Nope!"

"Yeah, we'll get you on some game shows!" Lucy said, ignoring him. "You'll solve math problems, or answer trivia questions, or spell big words no one's ever heard of, or...What's wrong? You look confused. I thought that didn't happen to smart people."

"That's because I'm not the smartest kid in class," William explained.

"That'd be me." Mason waved. "F-a-r-t, that spells 'smart'!"

"It does not," Olivia said. "Actually, I'm the smart one in this class. Possibly the only one." Olivia went back to doing long division—for fun.

"So what do you want to be famous for?" Lucy asked William.

"I want to be a famous rapper," William said.

Now it was Lucy who looked confused. She shrugged. "Okay, MC Willy, show me what you got."

William picked up a pencil, pretending it was a mic. He turned his hat sideways and did his rap:

"Yo, yo, yo!
My name is Willy,
and I'd like to say,
"I am a student in school,
in the Classroom THIRTEEN!

"Boom!" ~~MC Willy~~ William said. He dropped his pretend mic to the floor. No one applauded.

"You do realize raps are supposed to *rhyme*, right?" Lucy said.

Confused, William scratched his head. "They are?"

CHAPTER 18
Emma

When it was Emma's turn, something very strange happened. Lucy couldn't find her talent contracts, or her pen, or her purse. They had all vanished into thin air.

"I've been robbed!" Lucy screamed.

But as Lucy was about to have a panic attack, Emma revealed each of the missing items—by pulling them out of a top hat.

"Ta-da!" Emma said with a smile.

The room burst into applause.

"Bravo!" Mason shouted. "B-a-r-f, that spells 'bravo'!"

"No it doesn't." Olivia rolled her eyes.

Emma put the top hat on and took a small bow for Lucy. "I want to be a famous magician. I already know five good tricks, my assistant works for free, and I'm okay to travel coach to save on expenses."

And that's how the *Emm*-azing Emma was born. The Ace Agent Agency booked her at birthday parties and small theaters to see how well she'd perform. Emma nailed every show, wowing the audience with her five unbelievable illusions:

Trick 1: Emma could pull animals out of her hat. First, a rabbit. Then a bald eagle. And finally a lion. "Abracadabra!"

Trick 2: Emma could change stuffed animals into real animals. First, a bear. Then a giraffe. And finally a tiger. "Alakazam!"

Trick 3: Emma could blow bubbles through her fingers. Then she could make them into balloon animals. They were usually cats. "Sim-sala-bim-cat!"

Trick 4: Emma could remove her own head and bounce it on her arms. This usually made someone in the crowd faint. "Shazam!"

Trick 5: Emma could use her wand to make someone in the audience levitate—which means to rise or hover in the air. "Hocus-pocus!"

The *Emm*-azing Emma's popularity grew fast. Before she knew it, she was performing a SOLD-OUT show in Madison Square Garden. But before her show, a group of six strange adults walked into her dressing room.

"Who are you?" Emma asked.

"We are the secretive Magicka Society, a community of professional illusionists," said the short, squat man in a purple cape.

"We have seen your shows and would like you to join us," said a tall, thin woman who wore a red velvet cape.

"All you need to do is to tell us *how* you do your magic," said a rather large man wearing a cape of gold sequins.

"I'd love to join," Emma said. "I don't mind sharing, but there's nothing to share. It's just magic."

The Magicka Society didn't believe her. "Are you using mirrors to trick our eyes so that it looks like your head is off your shoulders?" one magician asked.

"It's a hologram! You're using computer and camera equipment! I saw a news story about this. With my mom. Who I still live with!" said another.

"No, no, no, you fools! It's a puppet! She uses a series of pulleys and strings to create her illusions!" said a third magician.

"Nope, nope, nope," Emma said. "It's just magic. Here, I can prove it!"

With a wave of her hand, the *Emm*-azing

Emma *poof*ed into a cloud of smoke, then reappeared on top of the large magician with a funny mustache. She took off her head and handed it to him.

"See? No mirrors, no computers, no strings," Emma's head said.

The society members freaked out, tossing her head from one to the other. Emma finally caught her head and put it back on.

"No fair!" the mustached magician said. "You're using *real* magic! You're a...a...a... WITCH!"

With torches, the six strange adults chased Emma onto the stage. "She's a witch! A witch!" they shouted to the crowd.

"Boo!" the crowd hissed. Apparently, people like fake magic. Not real magic. The *Emm*-azing Emma's professional magic career was over.

A single tear ran down Emma's cheek. Then she hopped on a broom with her rabbit and flew away.

CHAPTER 19
Liam

Lucy sniffed something and felt sick. She held her nose and waved away a fart cloud. "Did you do that?" Lucy asked.

"Guilty as charged," Liam said, tipping his Viking helmet to her. Liam stood there with a devilish grin and a milk mustache above his lip.

"I'll work with you, but you can't fart around me," Lucy said. "Understood?"

"Works for me. I may be able to fart the national anthem, but I don't want to be famous for farts. I've broken records, I've come back from the dead, and I used to breathe under-water. Everybody thinks they know what I'm going to do next, but I'm ready to shock them. Let's aim higher, like two hundred stories higher."

"Where are you going with this?" Lucy asked, already bored.

"Straight to the top of the world's tallest diving board, woman! And I'm taking the whole world with me!"

The stunt made national news. They showed images of a diving board two hundred stories in the air. On the ground was a swimming pool full of chocolate pudding. News reporters hovered, talking to their viewers like they were about to witness the greatest event in the history of humankind.

"In just a few short minutes, local legend Liam Lancaster, a young man who refuses to remove his Viking helmet, will attempt the impossible! A two-hundred-story belly flop into a pool of chocolate pudding! Will he survive?!"

"Absolutely," Liam said, starting his climb up the ladder. The first twenty stories were easy enough. He turned and flexed for the cameras, then waved to family and friends.

But by the time Liam reached fifty stories up, he began to feel nauseous. Maybe eating all those corn dogs right before wasn't the best idea. Liam tried to shake it off and kept climbing.

One thousand feet...one thousand five hundred feet...two thousand feet...the people looked like ants...and then smaller than ants...and then he couldn't see them.

As someone who rode roller coasters every chance he got, Liam never thought he'd be afraid of heights. But now the air was thinning at this height. The worst part was his hands wouldn't stop sweating. He had to be careful climbing the ladder.

When Liam finally reached the diving board, he clung to the rail. Then he looked down. Big mistake. The world was so far away. His knees knocked together. From the ground, people looked up with binoculars. It looked like Liam was doing a funny dance on purpose, but he wasn't. Liam was afraid.

Liam looked over the edge of the diving board. If he misjudged the angle of the belly flop, he'd be a pancake, and not the tasty kind. "I regret this decision!" he shouted to the wind.

Liam couldn't do it. It was just too...terrifying. He turned around to climb back down the ladder, just as a strong gust of wind blew his Viking helmet off his head! When he reached for it, he slipped.

Liam was now free-falling two hundred stories straight down!

As he fell, his life flashed before his eyes: It was just a series of wonderful, hilarious farts. Maybe he should go back to farts....

The ground got closer and closer...two thousand feet...one thousand five hundred feet...one thousand feet...five hundred feet...

Liam said his prayers. That's when the *Emm*-azing Emma—Classroom 13's only witch—flew straight toward him on her broom. Just as Liam was about to crash into the ground, Emma swooped in and caught Liam (and his Viking helmet). As they landed safely on the ground, Liam fainted—then farted.

"Gross," Emma said.

As his eyes slowly opened, Liam whispered, "That was fart for 'thank you.'"

CHAPTER 20
Fatima

"**A**re you an actress?" Lucy asked Fatima.

"Who, me?" Fatima said. "No."

"That's a shame because I told my movie studio friends I had an actress, but things didn't really work out with *him*."

"But they let me keep this!" Mason said, climbing back into the cardboard box like a kitten.

"Are you sure you're not an actress, kiddo?"

Fatima blushed. "No—but I'm really good at reading comics."

"Any interest in starring in a comic book movie?!" Lucy asked. "Those are all the rage right now!"

"*Comic book movie?!*" Fatima said, unable to hide her smile. She considered the possibilities....

No more cosplay with cheap costumes—she could wear a movie-grade supersuit. On-screen, she'd be a real superhero, blasting special-effects lasers out of her eyes or maybe even flying. She could be on panels with her favorite comic book movie characters. And best of all, she'd be the first to see her comic book movie—before anyone else!

"Ever heard of the *Super Squad?*" Lucy asked as she scanned emails on her phone. "They're looking for new cast members for the sequel."

"*Super Squad?!* It's only my favorite comic book movie of all time!" Fatima squealed with delight. "Count me in!!"

Amazingly, Fatima was cast in the sequel to her favorite movie. Not so amazingly, Fatima was *not* cast as a super*hero*—she was cast as a super*villain*.

She would be the evil Porcupina, the half-human, half-porcupine nemesis with spikes all over her body. This was terrible. Fatima hated Porcupina. So did most comic book fans. Porcupina sliced and diced their favorite heroes, and almost destroyed them on multiple occasions. She was cruel, awful, and just plain mean. She was the most sinister and deadly villain the *Super Squad* had ever faced in the comic books.

But this was Fatima's chance to meet the cast and be part of a superhero franchise. She couldn't pass it up. So she stayed her course and played the villainess. After filming had wrapped, Fatima and the rest of the actors from *Super Squad* were invited to San Diego Comic-Con.

As Fatima walked out on stage, the announcer said, "Introducing the bad girl you love to hate: Porcupina!"

But rather than clapping and cheering, the fans went crazy with rage. They booed and hissed, tossing half-eaten corn dogs at her. One fan even threw a Porcupina action figure. Its tiny plastic spikes really hurt!

Fatima was sad. No one at Comic-Con wanted a picture with her. Her costars were scared to be seen with her. She smelled like corn dogs. And worst of all, a mob of angry fans chased her out of the auditorium, shouting, "Stay away from our heroes, evildoer!"

"It's just a movie!" Fatima yelled. That only made the fans even more mad.

Fatima declined to go to the red carpet

premiere. Instead, she stayed home and watched the first *Super Squad* movie—alone.

Don't feel too bad for Fatima—she made a million dollars from the movie.

Then again, famous agent Lucy LaRoux took most of that.

CHAPTER 21

Mark

Everyone knew Mark was the most handsome boy in class. So when Lucy came to his desk, she immediately said, "Let's make you a model."

"Actually," Mark said, "I've always wanted to be a comedian."

"But you're so gorgeous," Lucy argued. "You're the universal idea of what beautiful looks like. I can make you the poster boy for just about anything."

"Yeah, but I don't want to be known for my good looks. I want people to know what's *inside*. That's what counts, right?"

Lucy started laughing. She kept laughing.

"What's so funny?" Mark asked.

"You *are* funny!" Lucy said. "But honestly, no one in Hollywood cares what's in your heart or your head—not unless you're a writer. Like Honest Lee. I represent him. And everyone likes his writing. Don't they?"

Mark and Lucy both looked right off this page and looked at *you*. What do you think of the writing?

CHAPTER 22
Zoey

Mark didn't want to be a model, but Zoey sure did. "Not just any model—I want to be a *super-model!*" Zoey said.

Lucy shook her head. "I'm sorry, gorgeous, but you're too short. Supermodels are tall." It was true. Supermodels are usually very tall, and Zoey was the shortest girl in Classroom 13.

"But it's my dream!" Zoey said.

"I once had a dream," Lucy said. "And life crushed it. That's why I became an agent. Do you want to be an agent? You could rep models."

Zoey thought of helping other people to become models while she remained a...*non*-model. The thought was too much for Zoey, and she began to cry. She buried her face in her hands—her soft, well-shaped, perfectly sized, beautiful hands.

"Those hands!" Lucy said. "They're stunning!" She took off her watch and handed it to Zoey. "Put this on!" Lucy told her, forcing the watch around Zoey's wrist.

Lucy gasped with awe. The watch had never looked better. It was a real-life vision that could be on a billboard over Sunset Boulevard. Zoey's hands were perfect for modeling rings, bracelets, gloves, and more.

"Kid, I take it all back. You *are* going to be a supermodel," Lucy said.

Zoey leapt up with excitement. "I am?!"

"Yes! A HAND model!"

Zoey was usually very picky and particular, but in this case, she didn't care. As her classmates cheered for her, Liam went in to high-five Zoey, but Lucy stopped him.

"Nuh-uh, Mister! Those hands are *never* to be touched. They are now Ace Agent Agency property." (So Liam high-fived himself.)

Lucy immediately took Zoey to get fitted for protective gloves. The pair of gloves were made of titanium metal on the outside and the softest silk on the inside. "These will keep your precious hands safe when you're not working," Lucy explained.

The following day, Zoey began her hand-modeling career. She modeled the newest watches, the most expensive rings, the craziest nail art, and a variety of lotions and hand soaps.

Zoey's hands became famous! Well, at least

on commercials. But her hands were working so much, Zoey never got a break. She liked being a model, but she did not like working. She was tired, and her hands were exhausted.

That night, when she got home, she went to put on her protective gloves. But they didn't fit. Zoey tried and tried to shove her fingers in there, but somehow, her hands were too big.

"I think my gloves shrank," Zoey told Lucy.

Lucy shrieked. "Your hands! Your glorious hands! What happened to them?! They're... they're *huge!*"

"They look the same, though," Zoey said.

"It doesn't matter. Little-girl hands sell products. Man hands don't."

Lucy tried to hide the problem. But on set, Zoey's hands were too big for the jewelry. The photographer took one look and said, "You can't model our dainty product with those meat hooks. You're fired. Sorry, not sorry."

"But, please, I can still model!" Zoey pleaded, trying to grab the photographer. Her hands were so strong that she crushed his camera without meaning to.

"I can fix it! I can still do this!" Zoey said.

"Talk to the hand," the photographer said, holding up his normal-sized hand, which was smaller than Zoey's. "Get off my set."

Lucy was about destroy Zoey's contract when she got a call. "Looks like I need a man-hands model. How do you feel about modeling boxing gloves, men's deodorant, and paper towels?" Lucy asked.

"Do I still get to be called a supermodel?" Zoey asked.

"Sure." Lucy shrugged. And that's how Zoey started her modeling career.

CHAPTER 23
Teo

"Let's get me famous," Teo said to Lucy as soon as it was his turn.

"And what's your talent?" Lucy asked.

Teo pulled out his phone and showed her his homepage. "I want to be a world-famous YouTube star," Teo said. "I have forty-seven followers, but I can do better. I have ideas. Lots of ideas."

"I like you, kid." Lucy smiled. "Let's get started."

Lucy followed Teo around for days and days and days. She recorded everything and uploaded it to social media. Then she had her other famous clients post and repost, again and again. In a matter of days, Teo had *forty-seven million* followers.

"Much better!" Lucy said. "But now we need to build your brand."

"My brand?" Teo said, confused. "But I'm already famous. I have forty-seven million followers."

"That's nothing! If you want to stay famous, you have to keep up the hard work," Lucy explained. "You need a *brand*. What makes you *you*?"

"Um, well, I like video games and movies and goofing around...."

"Perfect! That's your brand!" Lucy said.

So Lucy and the Ace Agent Agency camera crew followed Teo around. They filmed him playing video games, talking about his favorite movies, and goofing around on his skateboard.

But as Sunday rolled around, he remembered he had plans.

"Sorry, I can't film today," Teo said. "I have plans with my grandpa Walt. We're going kayaking and then mountain biking."

"Kayaking and mountain biking are *IN*," Lucy said. "But grandfathers are *OUT*. No one wants to see grandparents doing fun things."

"I do," Teo said.

"Do you want to be famous, or don't you?" Lucy asked.

Teo thought about it. "I really do like being a famous Internet star, but... well, famous is temporary, but family is forever."

As Teo walked away from his fame, he felt good about himself. When he went home, he and his grandfather made the funniest, most famous Internet video ever. It turned out Lucy was wrong about grandparents being *OUT*. They are very much *IN*.

CHAPTER 24
Chloe

"**R**eady to be famous and rich?" Lucy asked Chloe.

"Famous, yes," Chloe answered. "Rich, no."

Lucy didn't understand. But that's because she didn't understand Chloe.

Chloe cared deeply—about everything. She never met a can she didn't want to donate, or a tree she didn't want to plant, or a paper she

didn't want to recycle. Chloe loved her causes. Why? Because...

Chloe *cared*.

"I want to make the world a better place," Chloe explained to Lucy.

"I don't get you, kid," Lucy said.

"I have an idea. It's a nonprofit charity called the Care-plane Society," Chloe said. "Like *airplane*, only it's *Care*-plane, because we care—"

"Yeah, I got it," Lucy snipped.

"So what we do is the Ace Agent Agency buys an airplane, and I'll fill it with food and medicine and school supplies. Then we fly the plane all over the world, dropping off goods to those in need. We would put it up on social media and get people to donate food and medicine and school supplies. Or they can just donate money—"

That got Lucy's attention.

"I like money!" Lucy squealed. "Hmmm. I suppose this would be a huge tax break for the Ace Agent Agency. My boss will like that. Genius!"

"That's not what I meant," Chloe whispered. But she went along with it so that she could make the Care-plane idea into a real thing. People in need would have food and medicine and school supplies, and that's what really counted.

Chloe organized everything. There were places to drop off food, hospitals that would donate medicine, and large companies to provide free school supplies. But Chloe needed someone to run the website for money donations. She looked online and found a successful New York businessman to organize the donations. His name was Jeremiah Jerk.

"It's pronounced *Jerr*," he explained. "The *k* is silent."

Then Chloe and Lucy put together a huge celebrity bash to raise awareness about the Care-plane Society. Together, they raised millions and

millions of dollars. Chloe couldn't believe it. Her dream to help others was about to come true.

Only it wasn't.

It turns out Jeremiah *Jerr* really was Jeremiah *Jerk*, famous con man. He wasn't putting the money in the Care-plane Society's account. He was putting it into his own pockets. He stole the money, then stole the actual Care-plane. He flew it out of the country and didn't drop a single dollar, canned good, medicine, or school supply on anyone's head—rich or poor.

He was never heard from again.

The Care-plane Society was now penniless, planeless, and helpless. And Chloe—poor Chloe who cared so much—was known, *infamously*, as a thief.

CHAPTER 25
Earl

When Lucy came to Earl, she took one look at the class hamster and said, "Ew. It stinks. No celebrity potential there. I'm *not* going anywhere near that rodent."

Rodent?! Earl thought. He was *very* offended. He'd show that awful agent a thing or two....

CHAPTER 26
Mya & Madison

"**W**e want our own clothing line, our own perfume, and our own TV show," Madison & Mya explained to Lucy. No one in Classroom 13 wanted fame more than the twins.

"But what's your talent?"

"We don't have any," the twins said. (Remember what I said in Ximena's chapter, about every child having a talent? I meant that. But in this case, Mya & Madison were right. They didn't have any talents.)

"No talent?" Lucy smiled. "Then you're perfect for *reality TV*."

After school, Mya & Madison went home to find their house had been taken over by a TV crew. Camera guys and sound teams and makeup assistants wandered in and out of every room. There were even a bunch of writers.

"What do we need writers for?" the twins asked. "Isn't reality TV supposed to be based on reality?"

The writers all laughed. "In reality TV, *real* moments are all totally fake, scripted stuff we think up when we're on the toilet."

"Oh," Mya & Madison said, confused. They sat down at their desks to do their homework, like usual.

But the director stopped them and asked, "What are you doing?"

"Our homework."

"Nope. That's boring. This is reality TV. You need to spice it up," the director said. "People want to watch people fighting! Let's have the two of you fight over this pencil. And... roll the cameras. ACTION!"

The girls stood there, confused.

"But why would we fight over a pencil?" Mya said.

"We have more pencils in the drawer," said Madison.

"Pretend you don't!" the director growled.

"ACTIOOOON!" the director shouted again. "Roll the cameras. ACTION!"

The girls pretended to fight. Mya pretended to yell at Madison, and Madison pretended to keep the pencil away from her sister. But after a while, the twins forgot they were acting and started fighting for real. They screamed and pushed each other and pulled each other's hair. They even knocked over a table with their mom's favorite lamp. It broke into a thousand pieces.

"Perfect! I love it! Give me more!" the director called out.

So Mya & Madison gave him more—more fights, more arguments, and more tantrums. The girls were getting good at being mean to each other. But the moment the cameras turned off, they apologized and went back to loving each other.

Their reality show, *Mya & Madison: TWINning at Life!* was a huge success. The girls had their show, they had a new clothing line, and a new fragrance. The twin sisters felt like they had finally made it—

—until the gossip blogs online started making up stories about them. Some of the headlines included:

Madison Kills Alligator, Makes It Into Purse!

Mya Hires Orphans To Clean Bathroom Floors!

Reality Tv Twins Pour Oil On Penguins, On Purpose!

Mya & Madison, Not Real Twins!

Of course, none of that was true. (Well, Mya *did* hire some orphans to scrub her bathroom tub, but only because her mom insisted they still do their chores at home.) But it still hurt the girls that people *really* thought that about them.

When Mya & Madison felt like they couldn't take it anymore, Lucy taught them the harsh truth about reality TV: The negative press was part of why the show worked. Some fans hated to love them, and others loved to hate them. But the most important thing was that the people kept watching their show, no matter what.

Mya & Madison agreed. Being infamous wasn't so bad. So they kept fake-fighting for the cameras. It turns out they did have a hidden talent after all.

CHAPTER 27
Jacob

One kid in Classroom 13 knew TV better than he knew the freckles on the back of his hand. (Oddly enough, one of those freckles was shaped like a TV.) That kid was Jacob Jones.

Lucy sat on his desk and said, "I like your face. You should be on TV."

"I don't know," Jacob said. "I've had a taste of celebrity life, and it wasn't as great as I'd hoped.

You can't go anywhere without people recognizing and harassing you. It's kind of awful."

"What if you could be famous *without* people seeing your face?" Lucy asked with a sly smile.

"I'm listening...." Jacob said, intrigued.

"By any chance, do you like Mario's Meatballs & Spaghetti?"

"The ones that come in a can? I love it! I eat it for dinner all the time!" Jacob said.

And so Lucy cast Jacob in a commercial—but not as himself. He wore a costume that transformed him into a mascot for his favorite canned spaghetti. As Meatball Mario, Jacob became a singing, dancing stack of meatballs covered in spaghetti. His character would dance under a shower of Parmesan cheese and sing songs to entice kids to eat his canned goods. At the end of each commercial, fireworks would explode all around him as he said his tagline:

"Mario's Meatballs are magically mouthwatering!"

Jacob loved the idea. He got to be on TV during his favorite shows, but he didn't have to put up with any fans chasing him around town.

But after a few hours of actual work, Jacob could barely breathe. It was so hot inside the suit, he would sweat like a man crossing the Sahara without water. All that sweating made his face break out in pimples. And it made him stink, too. After filming, he didn't want to be seen— or smelled—in public. And when the fireworks went off, he almost always got burned.

Needless to say, Jacob wasn't happy.

"I can't keep doing this," Jacob told Lucy. "I've lost twenty pounds, I stink every day, and my face looks like a pizza."

"Do you want to do pizza commercials, too?" Lucy asked.

"No!" Jacob said. "I don't want this job anymore. It's not as fun as I thought it would be."

"Sorry, kid," Lucy said. "You signed a lifetime contract to appear in Meatball Mario

commercials. You'll be doing this for the rest of your life."

So, dear reader, the next time you see a funny commercial on TV with someone inside a costume, think of Jacob. You may be laughing at the commercial and enjoying yourself, but the actor inside that costume is sweaty and stinky and they are *not* having a good time.

That's TV for you.

CHAPTER 28
Olivia

As the resident know-it-all of Classroom 13, Olivia Ogilvy had a lot of thoughts about things. She had thoughts about Ms. Linda, opinions about her classmates, and even a theory that the 13th Classroom was alive...which is ridiculous. (Isn't it?)

To earn her fame, Olivia wrote all her thoughts down. It became a series of very popular books.

You may have heard of them. She wrote her books under a *pen name*. A pen name is a fake name that writers sometimes use to hide their true identity.

What's that? Did she write *this* series? *Um...* I don't know!

CHAPTER 29
Lily

Famous agent Lucy LaRoux's cell phone rang. She took one look at the caller ID and turned pale. "It's my boss." She gulped. She answered, "Hello?"

Judging by all the screaming coming from the phone, it did *not* sound like good news for her. In between bursts of shouting, the kids in Classroom 13 heard Lucy whisper:

"Yep...Uh-huh...I'm *so, so* sorry....I know, you're right....But it wasn't my fault....It will never happen again....I'm begging you....Okay, got it...Thank you...I won't let you down!"

Lucy turned off her phone and glared at the students of Classroom 13. "Is everything okay?" Ms. Linda asked her cousin.

"No, everything is *not* okay," Lucy said. "Right now, about half of your students have made me money, and the other half has cost me money. My boss is not happy. But we have one chance to make things right...."

Then Lucy got down on her knees in front of Lily. "You're the last student left. Please, please, *please* tell me that you're going to help me get a win for the Ace Agent Agency."

"Well, I want to be an astronaut, but I'm still too young. However, I do have all kinds of science-y ideas for inventions. For the last month, I've been building one to prank my four brothers...." Lily pulled the small device from her backpack. It looked like a little metal egg. "I call it the LILY-HAMMER 5000."

"What is it?" Lucy asked.

"It's an EMP," Lily answered.

The agent scratched her head. "Does that stand for: Egg Making Power?"

"No, it stands for Electromagnetic Pulse," Lily explained. "The Lily-Hammer 5000 emits an invisible pulse of EM energy that knocks out all electronics in a one-room radius. It makes TVs turn off, computers go to sleep, and phones shut down. But not forever. Everything will power back on again after an hour. I don't wanna break people's stuff; I just want to *prank* people.

"I've been doing it to my brothers all week. Every time they play their video games, I shut them down right before they beat a level. They have no idea it's me. It drives them nuts!"

"That's so cool!" said Yuna and Ava.

"That's so cruel!" said Dev and Teo.

"It looks like an egg, though," Lucy said. "Can it prank people *and* make eggs?"

"No," Lily said.

Lucy considered the egg-shaped machine. Even though she didn't quite understand it, Lucy did know that people liked technology and gizmos. "Okay, if that's the best you've got, let's see what I can do with it."

Lucy sent Lily's blueprints to the Ace Agent Agency. They filed a patent and started production immediately.

Pre-orders for the Lily-Hammer 5000® were in the millions. Pranksters of all ages couldn't wait to mess with their friends and families. The prank device cost three hundred bucks each, but no one cared. They wanted it.

The Ace Agent Agency was pleased with the sales numbers, and Lucy's boss told her she "did good." Things were looking up for Lucy and the Ace Agent Agency.

On the day it came out, Lily tried to turn on her computer. She wanted to read the reviews and the blogs and see what people thought of something she'd made. But her computer wouldn't turn on.

In fact, neither would her phone. Or her tablet. Or her TV.

Nothing worked.

That was because everyone in the country who bought a Lily-Hammer 5000 got their package shipped to them in the mail at the exact same time. That meant everyone in the country opened the package at the exact same time. That also meant everyone in the country turned on their own personal Lily-Hammer 5000 at the exact same time...

...and that created one giant EMP so massive it fried nearly every device in the country. No one could call or text or play silly games on their phones.

Everyone *freaked* out. Society went crazy. Many

believed it was a return to the technological dark ages. Needless to say, people were furious.

Lucy was so mad her face was the color of... well, I can't think of a metaphor, so let's just say her face was really, really *red*. "I thought you said the pranked phones would turn back on after an hour?" Lucy yelled.

"They were supposed to...." Lily said, rechecking her notes and calculations. "Oh, I see what happened. People weren't supposed to use their Lily-Hammers at the same time. We should have put a warning on the box."

"Now you tell me!" Lucy shouted. "I told you this thing should've made eggs!"

Technology in the country did not turn back on after an hour. Or twelve hours. Or twenty-four hours.

The Ace Agent Agency started getting letters—

actual letters, in the mail, with stamps. The letters were all complaints.

"How am I supposed to order a pizza without my cell phone?" one angry letter said. "I am starving!"

"How am I supposed to text my friend Jeff 'you are kewl' with a sunglasses emoji?" another angry letter said. "Now Jeff probably thinks I'm mad at him!"

"What am I supposed to do in the bathroom? Just use the bathroom?! I like to play games on the toilet! This is madness!" said a third letter (probably written while on the toilet).

Finally, the president declared a state of national emergency and demanded that people destroy their Lily-Hammer 5000s. To help people calm down, the president also bought everyone a new phone. After all, *she* was a very good president. (Yes, the president in this world is a woman, and she is a very good president at that!)

Then Madam President demanded the Ace Agent Agency refund everyone's money. Immediately.

Lily may have been embarrassed that her invention broke the country. But her embarrassment was nothing compared to the rage Lucy LaRoux was feeling at this moment. Lucy was in big trouble at her job, and Lucy needed to blame someone....

CHAPTER 30
Infamous Lucy!

On Friday, something occurred to Ms. Linda. "With all of you becoming famous and infamous, I honestly can't remember the last time we did any actual classwork," she said. "So... POP QUIZ!"

The students of Classroom 13 groaned. Some of the students were still famous (or *infamous*), but all of them still had to go to school. They prepared themselves for a boring, terrible, regular day of work, when—

—the door swung open, and a furious Lucy stormed in.

"*Stop whatever it is you're doing!*" Lucy shouted at them.

"Excuse me, Lucy LaRoux, but this is *my* classroom," Ms. Linda said. "You may be my cousin and a famous agent, but in here, I am in charge."

"No, no, no!" Lucy growled, stomping her feet on the floor and pitching a tantrum. "I have something to say, and all of you are going to listen!

"In all my time as a senior talent agent, I have *never* dealt with such horrible clients before! Look at all of you! Failed wrestlers and failed artists and failed actors—"

"I didn't fail. I quit," said Triple J.

"Same here," said Sophia.

"Me too," said Dev.

"When I say *fail*, I mean *failed to make me stinking rich*!" Lucy LaRoux screamed.

"Then you should have said so," Ms. Linda said. "After all, I don't think anyone in this class failed. I think everyone did a wonderful job."

"If they did such a wonderful job, then why is my job in jeopardy?!" Lucy asked.

"I suppose *our* goals and *your* goals were not in alignment—meaning, on the same path. If you feel the same way, perhaps you should nullify, or cancel, our contracts. Then all of us can go our separate ways, giving one another only well wishes," a voice said from the back of the class.

Everyone expected it to be Olivia (because of all the big words), but it turned out to be Mason.

Ms. Linda was impressed. She could hardly believe Mason—who believed Halloween candy was alive and could read his mind—formed such a structured and well-thought reply. It was *not* like Mason. "Mason, that was incredibly well spoken," she told him.

"Thank you," Mason said. "I hit my head this morning. My smarts will wear off soon. For now,

I'll return to my box." Mason climbed back into his empty box like a sleepy kitten.

"What is wrong with all of you?!" Lucy shouted. "You know what—it doesn't matter! You all work for me!"

She slammed their contracts down on Ms. Linda's desk. "None of you can just quit! I'll lose my job unless I make some real money off you kids, and that's just what we're going to do. You all signed these contracts, and contracts are *binding*, which means I *own* all of you! Kiss your families good-bye because you'll never see them again! You'll be too busy working for the rest of your lives! I don't care if you fulfill your contracts as celebrity toenail-clippers or circus pooper-scoopers or whatever other terrible jobs I can think of. You. Will. *WORK!*"

A hush fell over the class.

Some students started to cry. Others just got angry. They didn't like being famous *or* infamous. (And those who did like it really didn't like Lucy LaRoux—she had taken all their money and had yet to share the profits.)

"Now, listen here," Ms. Linda said. "You will *not* come into my classroom and bully these children. As far as I'm concerned, your contracts are already null and void."

With that, Ms. Linda took the stack of contracts and ripped them in half.

"YAAYYYY!" the students cheered. They'd never realized how awesome Ms. Linda was before now.

"Not so fast!" Lucy said with a sneaky sneer. "I have *copies*."

"BOOOOO!!" the students moaned.

But when Lucy opened her purse, she screamed. Earl crawled out with a fat belly and let out a long, rude *BURP*. He had gotten his revenge.

"That rodent ate my duplicates!" Lucy hissed.

"YAAYYYY!" the students cheered.

"No matter!" Lucy snapped. "I have *triplicates*!"

"BOOOOO!!" the students moaned.

But when Lucy opened her briefcase, the *Emm*-azing Emma snapped her fingers. The contracts *poof*ed into a cloud of purple smoke and glitter.

"Yay?" some of the students cheered. They weren't sure how many more copies Lucy LaRoux had.

And sure enough, Lucy smiled a wicked smile. "Good thing I have *digital* copies of the contracts on my phone! Hah!"

"Good thing I bought a Lily-Hammer," Ms. Linda said, grabbing something from her desk.

"Those are illegal!" Lucy said. "If you use one of those EMP Lily-Hammer things, you'll go to jail!"

"How silly of me. It's not a Lily-Hammer. It's just a regular hammer." Then Ms. Linda grabbed her cousin's phone and smashed it into a hundred little pieces.

Lucy's smile finally faded. All her copies were gone. There were no more contracts. The students of Classroom 13 were free once more.

Ms. Linda opened the door of Classroom 13 and pointed to the hallway. "I think it's time for you to go, Lucy LaRoux. We need to get back to learning."

Defeated, famous agent Lucy LaRoux scowled at the classroom and said, "You're all terrible, and you'll never be famous again!"

Little did Lucy know that the kids were already famous. This is the third book they've starred in. And they'll star in many more to come....

As they were no longer famous (or infamous), the students of Classroom 13 finished the school day like most students do—with some very *un*famous activities.

Instead of walking a red carpet, they walked the tiled classroom floor to turn in their homework.

Instead of signing autographs, they signed their names on quizzes and tests. And instead of smiling for cameras and journalists, they just smiled for their teacher, Ms. Linda, who had saved them from her terrible cousin.

Meanwhile, outside in the hall, famous agent Lucy LaRoux was kicking the 13th Classroom's door in anger. Like most living things, Classroom 13 did *not* like being kicked.

"*Stop it,*" whispered the classroom door.

Lucy looked around. "Who said that?"

"*I did,*" said the voice.

Lucy looked up and down the hallway, but there was no one around. Just her. And the door to Classroom 13.

"*Don't kick me again,*" the door said. "*It's rude.*"

Lucy figured this was some kind of prank. She roared, "I'll do what I want!"

Then she kicked the door again. This time, her leg went right through the door. Lucy tried to pull her leg back, but it was stuck in what felt like strawberry jelly. Then, like a strand of spaghetti, the door sucked her in completely. She was not in Classroom 13. She was somewhere...*else*.

"*You should have made me famous,*" the 13th Classroom whispered. Then the door burped her out.

Lucy bounced into the hallway covered in slime. She had no idea what had happened or where she had been—but she was totally freaked. She ran out of the school, screaming and vowing to never work with children again.

Meanwhile, Ms. Linda and the students didn't hear a thing inside the 13th Classroom. They never did. But they would one day, one day rather soon....

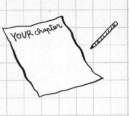

CHAPTER 31
Your Chapter

That's right—it's your turn!

Grab some paper and a writing utensil. (Not a fork, silly. Try a pencil or pen.) Or if you have one of those fancy computer doo-hickeys, use that. Now tell me...

What do YOU want to be famous for?

When you're done, share it with your teacher, your family, and your friends. (Don't forget your pets! Pets like to hear stories, too.) You can even ask your parents to send me your chapter at the address below.

HONEST LEE

LITTLE, BROWN BOOKS FOR YOUNG READERS

1290 Avenue of the Americas

New York, NY 10104

31901060949395